# Lola the Orca Lived at the Aquarium by the Sea

Everyone loved Lola
She put on a fabulous show
She flipped, jumped, waved to the audience with her tail and
even let her trainer ride her like a surfboard!

# Lola

## The Lonely Orca

CORINNA AHLSTROM

PAGE PUBLISHING, INC.
New York, NY

First originally published by Page Publishing, Inc. 2017

ISBN 978-1-68409-483-7 (Paperback)
ISBN 978-1-68409-484-4 (Digital)

Printed in the United States of America

The music played
The fireworks boomed
The audience cheered
All for Lola, she was a star!

One evening the
shows were over, and the audience went home.
All was quiet at the aquarium
when Madi, the owner's daughter,
walked by Lola's tank.

Madi noticed Lola looking very sad.
"What's wrong, Lola?"
"I am SO lonely." Lola sighed

"How could you possibly be lonely, Lola? People come from all over the world to see you perform your amazing tricks! It looks like you have such a glamorous life!" Madi exclaimed.

"Things are not always how they seem Madi.
I miss my mom and the rest of my Orca family.
We are called Pods and Orcas stay with their pod
their entire lives!"

"Wow! Your whole
life?" asked Madi.
"Yes! We stay together as
long as we live," said Lola.

"Oh no!" cried Madi.
"I can't imagine being taken away
from my mom and family."
"But it's so pretty here at the
aquarium, don't you like your home?"

"The ocean is my only home, Madi.
This tank may be fun for humans to look at, but
Orcas swim one hundred miles a day in the ocean."

"Humans may think I live the life of a superstar... But I don't want to be a star. It doesn't only hurt my heart to be away from my pod. But all the loud noises hurt my head too!"

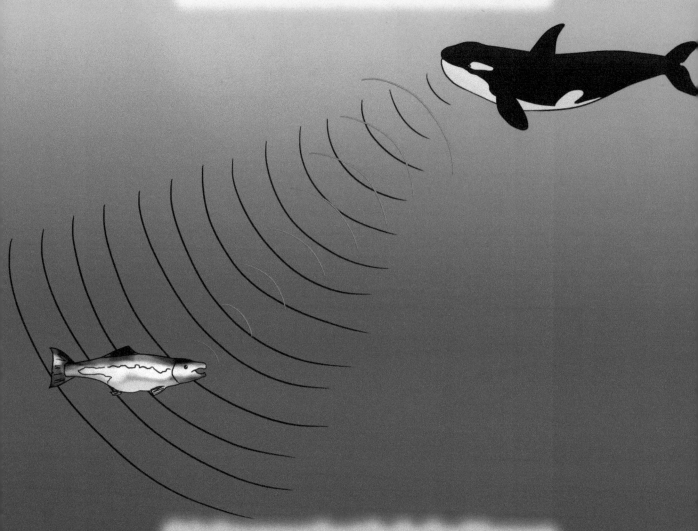

"I am an Orca.
My ears are not like yours, they are stronger, much more sensitive.
We have built in sonar called echo-location.
Echo-location bounces sound off objects, fish or other mammals.
Then we wait for the echo to come back!

It is the way we hunt for food and how we
are able to tell how close things are."
"That's so cool!" exclaimed Madi.
"It is!" Lola said proudly.

"But I was brought here to be a performer, and as they say in show business, the show must go on," Lola said sadly.

Suddenly, Madi's face lit up with a
twinkle of hope
"Lola, I am going to help you go
home to your family."

Weeks passed, and it was life as usual at the aquarium

9:00 hand-fed breakfast

10:00 rehearsal

11:00 show time

1:00 hand-fed lunch

2:00 rehearsal

3:00 show time

5:00 hand-fed dinner (sigh)

Day after day, the same routine.

Then one morning Madi came running to Lola's tank
"WE DID IT. WE DID IT. YOU ARE GOING HOME TO
YOUR FAMILY."
My dad is turning this aquarium into a marine
animal rescue center and seaside sanctuary.
Lola's eyes perked up.
"What is a seaside sanctuary?" asked Lola

A seaside sanctuary is a cove in the ocean
but still protected.
You will be able to feel the ocean's
currents, dive down to deep water to fish
and to call for your pod.
We will watch over you until your mom
comes to get you!

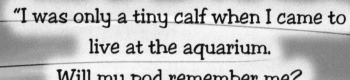

"I was only a tiny calf when I came to
live at the aquarium.
Will my pod remember me?
Will they hear my calls?" Lola thought to herself.
Lola was overwhelmed with emotion as she waited.

Lola can see a huge crane
driving toward her with a
sling attached; it looks like a big blanket.
"I'm so scared, Madi." Lola
shook in her tank.
"It's going to be just fine, a
little ride up in the air, and
they will swing you over to the ocean.
My dad and I will meet you there!"

The men lowered the sling into Lola's tank.
She bravely swam toward it as
her trainers buckled her in
for her short journey to the seaside sanctuary.

Lola kept her eyes shut as she was being lifted
away from the chlorine-filled pool that stung
her eyes and made it hard to breathe.
She can smell a change in the air.
The wind shifted, and suddenly,
there was an old familiar scent.
The salty air of the ocean
Lola was headed "home."

The crane drove a bit,
and she can feel it
swinging her another direction.
She opened her eyes; she
could see the dark
blue water of the ocean,
and it didn't stop,
no sides to this "tank"
the sea "went on
forever," Lola thought to herself.

Down she went to the seaside sanctuary,
just as Madi promised!
Her excitement grew as the crane lowered her
down to the water.

Lola's anxiety was eased as soon as she felt the cool
water of the ocean. It felt amazing!
Her trainers were waiting at the bottom to unbuckle her.

As the sling went deeper into the water,
Lola was able to wiggle herself out of it and into the cove.
She can feel the ocean's currents; she was
able to fish for herself like Orcas do,
and for the first time in years, Lola was able to hear other sea life
interacting with each other. She heard a
dolphin family as they swam by,
which reminded her
"I can call my pod; I hope they hear me."
She called to her mom,
she called to her dad,
she called to her brothers and to her sisters ...
someone has got to hear me
"I'm free, I'm free... so excited for my pod to come get me!
The excitement made her jump for joy!"

Lola swam as fast as a race car
around the cove, then dove right to the bottom,
turned around and breached the water!
She jumped, flipped and splashed all around the seaside
sanctuary, not because a trainer made her
because she wanted to.
She suddenly heard a friendly voice call her name from the shore,
"Lola!"

Lola spotted Madi standing with her dad on the rocks
by the shore and swam to them
"I called my pod, even if they are many miles away;
they will hear me," Lola said with a twinkle in her eyes
Madi reassured Lola, "They will come."

Madi reached her hand out and put it against Lola's face.
"Please don't forget me Lola," Madi cried.
How could I ever forget you, Madi? You are my best friend!
You were my voice when no one else could hear me;
You fought for me when I couldn't fight for myself.
You are the bravest person I know!
Madi, you prove that no matter how small the person,
they can still make a huge difference
YOU are MY hero, Madi!

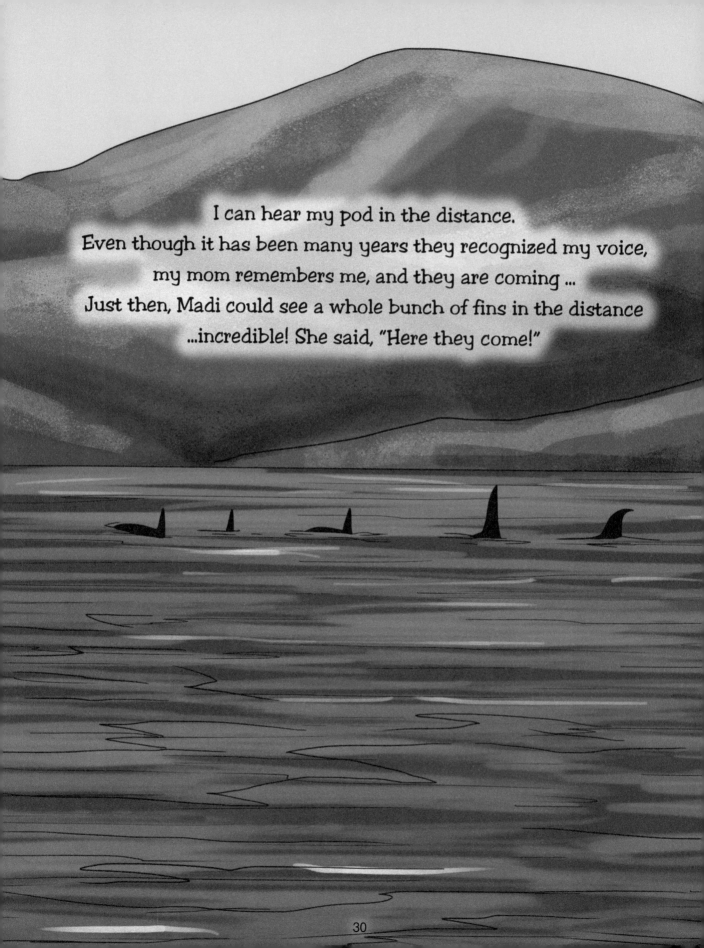

I can hear my pod in the distance.
Even though it has been many years they recognized my voice,
my mom remembers me, and they are coming ...
Just then, Madi could see a whole bunch of fins in the distance
...incredible! She said, "Here they come!"

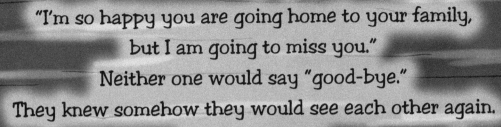

"I'm so happy you are going home to your family,
but I am going to miss you."
Neither one would say "good-bye."
They knew somehow they would see each other again.
I love you, Lola
I love you too, Madi.
Lola isn't lonely anymore. ♥

For the whales.

# About the Author

Cori Ahlstrom is an animal and marine life advocate giving voices to those who don't have one, with hope to spread awareness about captivity and animal cruelty. Helping the next generation to be better humans and leave the earth a kinder place.

CPSIA information can be obtained
at www.ICGtesting.com
Printed in the USA
LVHW072315100720
660358LV00005B/160